Everybody loves a scary mystery story. Now you can enjoy
tales that come with a good dose of fright, lots of suspense and
a bit of humour too! Mysteries books are sure to have
you spooked!

Read on if you dare!

DETECTIVES OF THE IMPOSSIBLE

Sherlock Holmes is a hero. He is the Great Detective. People have been reading about his adventures for years. He can solve the most puzzling mysteries from the tiniest of clues. Nothing is impossible to him.

BUT — could Sherlock solve the weird, modern mysteries in these books? Could he work out how a passenger disappears from a plane that's flying 30,000 feet in the air? Could he solve the puzzle of how a person seems to shrink to microscopic size? Would he crack the cases of a dead body that falls out of an empty cabinet, or how someone is poisoned inside a locked room? Read on and see if you can outdo Sherlock by solving these mysteries yourself. Or . . . are they simply impossible?

CONTENTS

Chapter One

AN ANXIOUS COACH RIDE

"Are we there yet?"

Thirteen-year-old Mateo Rivera peered through the bus window at the Canadian countryside passing by. But all he could see was the single-lane road and the thick pine trees on either side of it.

"Dude, chill," his friend Lola said. She sat slumped next to Mateo in the seat. Her plait was twisted on top of her head like a piece of art. In her hands, she spun a multi-coloured cube in different directions to line up the colours. She placed a hand on Mateo's bouncing knee. "You're gonna make *me* nervous."

"You're not nervous?" Mateo asked. "We came all the way here from Florida to compete in a puzzle competition against the smartest kids in the world." He glared at Lola with wide eyes. "The *world*, Lola!"

Lola shrugged. "It'll be fun." She blew a large bubble from the gum she was chewing, popped it, and went back to her game.

Mateo glanced around the small coach. Other kids about their age filled the plush blue seats. Some read books; others played games on their handheld devices. They had come from more than thirty countries. Each kid had received the same exciting email that he and Lola got after applying for the competition.

Mateo's knee began to bounce again.

The coach turned onto a gravel road. Ahead was a wooden archway over the road. It held a large banner that read in bold red letters:

WELCOME TO CAMP ENIGMA,

HOME OF THE INTERNATIONAL

TWIST! PUZZLE COMPETITION!!!

The mood on the coach became energetic as all the kids saw the sign.

"We're here," Mateo whispered to Lola, who hadn't seemed to notice the excitement in the air.

Lola smiled, flipped the cube into her open backpack and zipped it up.

The coach rumbled down the gravel road, kicking up a stream of dust between the pine trees on either side. When they passed beneath the sign, a cheer rang out.

Soon the trees spread apart, and a campsite appeared in front of the coach. The driver honked as he pulled to a stop in front of the main lodge. The door hissed open, and the kids grabbed their things, noisily filing off one by one.

Mateo leapt off the top step of the coach and landed in the grass with a soft thump. He looked around. The campsite was in a large clearing. Small wooden cabins dotted the area. Behind them was a crystal blue lake.

Mateo was used to the ocean. He enjoyed the crashing waves and the warm, wet sand on the Florida beach. But this was something else. It was peaceful. Mateo had never seen such a large space that was so quiet before.

The kids from the coach huddled together nearby. As Mateo and Lola joined them, a man came thundering over.

"Gooood afternoooon!" The man was heavyset, with wild silver hair and a matching beard. He held out his arms and smiled at the kids. "What a great turnout we have this year! I'm Thaddeus Maxwell, and I'll be your host and judge for this unforgettable weekend!"

Mr Maxwell spun around and began to stride away, waving for the others to follow. "Come along!" he said. "Let me show you around our lovely camp!" The throng of excited kids quickly followed in Mr Maxwell's enormous shadow.

"This place is so . . . quiet," Mateo said to Lola.

"I know. Isn't it great? I love the woods," Lola replied. "Come on, let's keep up."

The two friends slung their backpacks onto their shoulders and hurried after the group.

Chapter Two

CAMP ENIGMA

Thaddeus Maxwell guided the *TWIST!* competitors around the campsite. "Over there is the mess hall where we'll eat our meals." He pointed a meaty finger at a long brick building. The building next to the mess hall had a welcome banner similar to the one hanging over the road. "And that's where we'll host the competition tomorrow," Maxwell explained.

He next led them to the row of cabins near the lake. Kayaks and canoes leaned against a wooden shed near the shoreline. As Mateo gazed across the lake, he noticed a small island in the middle of the lake. *Not exactly an island*, he thought. He could barely make out a narrow strip of land that led from the forest out to the island.

"You'll each be given a bunk in one of our cabins," Mr Maxwell said. His booming voice brought Mateo back to the moment. "This first one, the only single-person cabin, goes to Reza Amari."

A wiry boy with shaggy black hair and braces on his teeth stepped out of the crowd. "*Of course* Reza gets his own cabin," Lola said in Mateo's ear. "He won last year's *TWIST!* competition, and he's the front-runner to win *this* year too."

"Thank you, Mr Maxwell," Reza said confidently.

"Now, let me show the rest of you to your cabins," Mr Maxwell said.

Mateo was placed in a cabin with five other boys. The cabin was small, with a fireplace and three sets of bunk beds. Mateo claimed one of the bottom bunks.

"Hey! Who wants to go swimming?" Conner, a short boy with a thick Australian accent, asked.

"Great idea!" a second boy, Henri, from France, replied.

Soon, the group was walking out of the cabin in their swimming costumes with towels draped over their shoulders. They weren't the only ones with the same idea though. Other boys and girls were already splashing in the lake.

There was one person, however, who was *not* going in the water. "Not a chance," Reza said when Conner asked him to join them.

"Oh, come on, Reza," Henri insisted. "It'll be fun."

Reza shook his head. "I *despise* water. I won't go near it."

Conner shrugged. "Suit yourself, mate," he said.

"Strange dude," Henri said as Reza walked to his cabin. Then the boys raced to the lake.

That evening, they ate grilled hamburgers and hot dogs in the mess hall. Mateo found Lola, and they sat together.

"Come over here, everyone!" Thaddeus Maxwell shouted as the kids finished their meals. "I've got a campfire roaring, and the marshmallows won't eat themselves!"

The sunset over the lake turned the clouds to brilliant shades of purple and orange. It was a stunning sight. A campfire flickered high into the sky in the middle of the campsite. The kids gathered around it.

Mateo saw Reza near Mr Maxwell. The boy seemed in much better spirits than before dinner. "Everyone have a seat!" Mr Maxwell said. The kids sat on tree stumps and in the grass around the fire. Lola found a log with enough room for two and motioned Mateo to join her.

Reza, however, remained standing.

Mr Maxwell began. "Let me officially welcome all of you to the Fifth Annual *TWIST!* Competition. You've each been invited here to compete in a variety of mental challenges. We'll have memory puzzles, maths games, logic experiments, riddle contests and more!

"You'll earn points based on how you perform in each challenge. Then at the end of the weekend we'll add up your scores, and the camper with the highest total points will be our big winner. And of course, it wouldn't be a *TWIST!* competition without a *twist!* So be ready for the unexpected.

"Now I have the pleasure of introducing last year's winner," Mr Maxwell continued. "Let's give a big hand to Reza Amari!"

"Thank you, Mr Maxwell. If I could have everyone's attention," Reza said, after the applause slowed down. "Mr Maxwell kindly agreed to let me tell you all a campfire story tonight. Would you all like to hear it?"

A rousing "Yes!" went up around the campfire.

Reza sat and rubbed his hands together. "Good. Because this one is scary." He paused, then added, "And it took place right here in the woods around Camp Enigma!"

Chapter Three

THE LEGEND OF THE WERE-SQUATCH

Darkness settled around the campers. Firelight danced in Reza's eyes.

"What I'm about to tell you happened long ago," he started. "It's the legend of a creature known as the were-squatch."

Whispers and giggles coursed like a wave through the gathered kids. "That can't be a real thing," Lola muttered. Mateo ignored her.

"Part wolf, part ape-like beast, the terrifying were-squatch lives in the woods outside the camp," Reza continued. "If you listen hard, you can still hear its unique howl."

Everyone grew quiet. The crackling fire was the only sound. Conner looked doubtfully towards the woods. Even Mr Maxwell, standing behind Reza with his hands in his sweatshirt pockets, seemed uncomfortable.

"The creature's size wasn't the only thing that frightened campers," Reza said. "It had beady yellow eyes that glowed in the moonlight. And if you were caught in its gaze . . ." Reza shook his head.

"What would happen?" Henri asked.

Reza held up two fingers, then slowly pinched them together. "The were-squatch's stare could shrink a person down to nothing."

"No way," Lola said.

In the distance, thunder rumbled. A storm was coming, making the mood even creepier.

"It happened during a night just like this," Reza continued. "A boy heard a howl

in the woods and raced out from his cabin to investigate."

"That makes no sense," Lola said. "Why would he run *towards* the sound?"

Reza smiled and raised an eyebrow. "I was hoping one of you master puzzlers would ask that. Sometimes, a person actually runs *towards* what they're afraid of, not *away* from it."

"So what happened to the boy?" Conner asked in a whisper.

"He ran through the woods until he stumbled right into the were-squatch! Later when others searched for the boy, all they ever found was a pair of muddy footprints. They grew smaller and smaller until they completely disappeared."

As if on cue, a high-pitched, throaty howl echoed from the middle of the woods. "Did you hear that?" Mateo asked Lola.

She nodded, squinting. "Yeah."

Just then a streak of lightning shot across the sky, followed by a clap of thunder. Kids shrieked in surprise. Mr Maxwell pulled his hands from his pockets. "I think that's enough storytelling for tonight, Reza," he said. "Let's hurry along back to our cabins and save the marshmallows until *after* tomorrow's competition."

The kids dashed off. As Mateo passed Reza, the dark-haired boy shouted to the group, "Perhaps tonight is a good night to lock your doors!"

A while later Mateo was laying in his bunk and staring at the bed above him. The boys around him turned restlessly in their bunks. Raindrops plunked on the roof and the cabin's windows. Mateo thought about texting Lola, but she clearly didn't believe Reza's story. And she would certainly make fun of him if he hinted that he did believe it.

* * *

Mateo must have dozed off, because the next thing he knew, a shaft of sunlight cut through the window and into the cabin. He got up, dressed, and joined his cabin mates as they walked towards the mess hall for breakfast. The ground was wet. Small puddles covered the campsite's pathways.

As they reached the mess hall, Mr Maxwell came bustling out. "Excuse me!" he shouted. "Has . . . has anyone seen Reza this morning?"

The group of kids outside shook their heads.

"He hasn't been to breakfast yet," Mr Maxwell said. "I hope he's okay." The large man strode across the campsite, heading for Reza's cabin. A large crowd, including Mateo and his cabin mates, followed Mr Maxwell. The man pounded on the door.

"Reza?!" he exclaimed. "Please open up!"

There was no response.

A worried look crossed Mr Maxwell's face. He tried the door. "Locked," he said. Then, surprisingly, he slammed his shoulder into the door. It sprang open.

Mr Maxwell gasped. "He's . . . he's missing!"

Chapter Four

THE DISAPPEARING
FOOTPRINTS

"My word!" Mr Maxwell said. "It appears there was quite a scuffle in here."

The kids pressed forward to see into Reza's cabin. Henri shoved Mateo from behind and stood on his tiptoes to look through the open doorway. "Not just a scuffle. This place was ransacked," Henri said.

Mr Maxwell stepped away from the open cabin. "Come along," he said anxiously. "We must call the authorities."

Mateo's heart skipped a beat. *The police?*

A short while later, a police car pulled into the campsite. The kids had been sent to wait in the mess hall. Some sat at tables gossiping while others whispered about how the competition would probably be cancelled. A few even talked about how they wanted to solve Reza's mysterious disappearance.

Many, like Mateo and Lola, stood at the window. They peered out as two police officers, a man and a woman, climbed out of the police car. Mr Maxwell stood near the door of Reza's cabin. Mateo noticed he kept looking at the mess hall.

He's probably worried about the rest of us, he thought.

"Huh," Lola said. "That's weird."

Mateo looked over. Lola twirled her plait in one hand. "What?" he asked.

"That female officer. She looks familiar."

"Familiar?" Mateo glanced at the officer. She had shoulder-length blonde hair and an angular face. She almost looked like a model. But she didn't look familiar to Mateo.

"Lola, we're 1,500 miles from home," he said.

"That's why I said it's 'weird', dude."

They watched the officers talking to Mr Maxwell. Then the trio walked to his cabin and went inside, most likely to call Reza's family. At that point many of the kids lost interest and wandered away from the window.

Mateo took Lola by the wrist. "Follow me," he said.

"Where are we going?"

"To get a look at that cabin."

Mateo led Lola out of a side door in the kitchen. They slipped across the clearing, easily making it to Reza's cabin without being seen.

The splintered front door was still open. Mateo and Lola peeked in, and what they saw gave Mateo goosebumps. Everything in the cabin had been turned upside down. The bed was messed up. A tall lamp lay tipped over by the window. A can of red paint was spilled in the middle of the room. And coming from the paint were—

"Footprints," Mateo said. A perfect pair of footprints emerged from the paint puddle, as if someone had stepped in it and ran towards the door. But there was something odd about the prints. "Look. The closer the prints get to the door . . ." Mateo started.

". . . the smaller they get," Lola finished Mateo's thought.

"They shrink," Mateo said. "Just like the ones in Reza's campfire story."

"Oh please," Lola said. "You don't really believe that nonsense, do you?"

Mateo didn't have time to answer. Mr Maxwell and the police officers had appeared behind them. "What do you think you're doing in here?" Mr Maxwell asked, his deep voice surprising Mateo.

"We just wanted . . ." Mateo's voice trailed off.

"Get back to the mess hall," Mr Maxwell instructed. He glanced around nervously at the trees around the cabin.

Does he believe the were-squatch legend too? Mateo wondered. *Or does he know more about Reza's disappearance than he's saying?*

As they walked away from Reza's cabin, Mateo turned to Lola. "I don't know what's going on," he said. "But there's one thing I *do* know. We need to keep an eye on Mr Maxwell."

Chapter Five

THE HOLLOW TREE

As the sun climbed higher into the late morning sky, the campers were allowed to go back to their cabins. Those who thought the were-squatch story was rubbish found their way to the kayaks and canoes on the lake. Some even kicked a football around. But the more cautious campers hid out in their cabins.

Mateo and Lola did neither.

They watched as Mr Maxwell helped the

police officers string tape across Reza's cabin door. Mateo noted their camp host's odd behaviour. Mr Maxwell first stared up into the trees and then out at the lake. Then he fumbled in his pocket for an envelope, which he passed to the officers. The female officer took the envelope and slipped it into her pocket.

"I can't stop wondering why she looks so familiar," Lola said.

As the police car drove off, Mr Maxwell walked back to his cabin. Mateo and Lola followed him, slinking behind trees and cabins. But as Mr Maxwell reached his office, he suddenly turned back.

Lola pushed Mateo towards the woods, onto a small, winding path.

"This way," she said. "Before he sees us."

"I guess we'll have to find another time to follow him," Mateo said.

The two friends walked side by side through the trees. Even in the broad light of day, the idea of a strange creature lurking in the woods gave Mateo the creeps.

"I think we should head back to the cabins," he said.

Lola picked up a rock and threw it into the bushes. "Why?" she asked, smirking. "Afraid of the were-squatch?"

"Well, *yeah*, kind of," Mateo answered honestly.

"Maybe Reza isn't really missing at all," Lola said. "Maybe he went home and didn't want to tell Mr Maxwell. I mean, is his family even on their way here?"

Mateo shrugged. There was definitely something odd about Reza's disappearance, but he couldn't put his finger on it. He thought of the other campers in the mess hall who said they'd love to solve the mystery. He would too.

Lola picked up another rock and chucked it into the woods.

Thunk.

"What was that?" Lola asked.

"I don't know."

The two left the path and walked through the trees. Fallen twigs and dead leaves crunched under their shoes. Soon, they found the large stone Lola had thrown. Next to it was a fallen tree trunk. Except there was something odd about the bark on it.

"This isn't a tree trunk at all," Lola said.

She was right. On closer inspection, the trunk was made of plastic. It was painted to look like a real tree. Black mesh covered one end. On one side was a housing for batteries and an "On/Off" switch.

"This looks like a remote speaker," Mateo said.

"In the middle of the woods?" Lola asked. "Why put it out here?"

"Another mystery about Camp Enigma," Mateo muttered.

But then it hit him. A mysterious *plastic* log in the woods. A camper missing from a locked cabin. A shifty camp director . . . it suddenly all made sense.

His eyes grew wide, and he clutched Lola's arm. "Lola," he said excitedly. "*This* is the real competition!"

"What?"

"Remember what Mr Maxwell said yesterday? Reza's disappearance is the twist! This whole thing is a locked-room mystery!"

Chapter Six

THE MYSTERIOUS MR MAXWELL

"A what?" Lola asked.

"A locked-room mystery," Mateo explained. "It's a real-life puzzle. Something happened to Reza. But his cabin was locked *from the inside*. So how did he disappear?"

Recognition dawned on Lola's face. "So you think Mr Maxwell—"

"–is playing a game with us!" Mateo exclaimed. "And if we solve the mystery, then we'll win the *TWIST!* contest!"

"That's it!" Lola snapped her fingers, then dug into her pocket and pulled out her phone. At first, Mateo thought she was making a call, but when she flipped the screen so he could see it, a video was playing.

Mateo read the colourful title on the screen. Yellow letters drifted in a cloudy blue sky to spell out *Where the Wind Blows*. He had no idea where she was going with this.

"It's one of my mum's favourite soap operas," Lola said. "It's filmed here in Canada. And one of its stars . . ."

She scanned through the video intro that showed the actors in the soap opera. She paused it on a pretty blonde woman called Kylie Rutherford. "There!" Lola said.

It took Mateo a second, but when he saw it, he gasped. "The police officer!" he hissed.

"She's not a real police officer at all," Lola explained. "She's an actress!"

"Then why was she here this morning?" Mateo wondered.

"Because you're right. Reza's disappearance is all part of an act."

"We need to try spying on Mr Maxwell again," Mateo said.

They made their way out of the woods near Mr Maxwell's office. The door was closed. One peek in the window confirmed he wasn't inside. All Mateo saw was a cluttered desk, a worn brown leather chair and an open cupboard with a bulky garment bag hanging on a hook.

"It's close to lunch," Lola said. "Maybe he's with the rest of the group."

Sure enough, as they headed back towards the cabins, Mateo spied Mr Maxwell walking towards the mess hall. He was alone and speaking into a walkie-talkie. He disappeared into the kitchen's back door, the same one Mateo and Lola had sneaked out of earlier in the day.

A narrow horizontal window was set high in the wall, above a stack of firewood. Mateo climbed up the stack of wood until he could see through the window.

"What's going on?" Lola began to climb up next to him.

In the kitchen, Mr Maxwell gathered items of food into a paper bag. Apples, bananas, a loaf of bread and a jar of peanut butter.

But why? Mateo wondered.

Lola reached the top of the woodpile and peered in. But as she went up on her tiptoes, the wood under her feet began to wobble.

"Whoa!" Lola teetered forwards. Her hand struck the window pane in front of her. The pane wiggled around in its frame but didn't fall out. Lola, however, fell off the woodpile and hit the ground hard.

"Oof!"

"Lola!" Mateo leaped down to help her. Panic raced through him. The noise was surely enough to get Mr Maxwell's attention. They had to get out of there!

"Are you okay?" he asked.

Lola nodded.

Mateo pulled her to her feet. "Good. Then *run!*"

Chapter Seven

A NIGHT-TIME INVESTIGATION

Mateo and Lola dashed away, not daring to look back. Mateo didn't hear the kitchen door open. And he didn't hear Mr Maxwell call out to them. So maybe they were safe?

They ducked behind a patch of raspberry bushes and lay flat on the ground. "Do you think he saw us?" Lola asked.

Mateo shook his head.

They waited behind the bush until they were sure the coast was clear. Mateo stood and peered back at the mess hall. Mr Maxwell was nowhere in sight.

"Maybe we should cool it on the investigation for a while," Lola said. "We could be wrong about the competition."

Mateo shook his head. "No," he replied. "This is all a test. And we're gonna solve the mystery. Tonight, we're going back to Reza's cabin to look for clues. Okay?"

Lola nodded. "Even if there happens to be a were-squatch on the loose?"

Mateo rolled his eyes.

Dinner that evening was eerily quiet. After the day's events, it seemed like many of the campers just wanted to go home.

"Sure didn't expect to fear for my life when I got to come here!" Conner stated loudly.

Mateo and Lola ate in silence while watching the sun set through the mess hall window. After dinner, the two friends split up to return to their cabins.

But as Mateo walked back alone in the dark, the sound of a howl cut through the clear night sky. He shivered in fright and glanced towards the woods. He half expected to see a pair of beady yellow eyes staring back at him. But there was only darkness.

Mateo hurried faster towards his cabin. But before reaching it, a hand reached out and grabbed his arm. He gasped in fright and then noticed that it was Lola. Mateo shook free from her grasp.

"Did you just–?" he gasped

"Pffft, ha!" she said, grinning. "Calm down, fraidy cat. I got you so good. So what's the plan?"

Mateo took a deep breath. "We'll stop at the supply shed first. I'll bet there are torches inside that we can use. From there, we go to Reza's cabin. Got it?"

The two teens carefully made their way along the edge of the woods, staying in the shadows. When they reached the shed, the lock appeared to be bent. "Someone broke into this shed recently," he whispered.

He pushed the door, and it opened with a soft creak.

The two slipped inside, closing the door behind them. In the dim moonlight they found a pair of heavy-duty torches. Mateo clicked one on and flashed the beam around. It landed on a nearby shelf.

"Check it out," he said.

The dusty shelf was smudged with handprints. Lola picked up a fallen jar and studied it. "It's a bunch of putty," she said. "Like the stuff that seals up windows."

"Odd," Mateo said. "And someone was just using it."

"How can you tell?" asked Lola.

Matteo held the jar closer in the beam of the torch. "See that bit of putty on the lid? It's still spongy. If it had been there more than a couple of days, it would be hard and dry."

The two friends left the shed. They kept to the shadows to avoid being seen and tiptoed towards Reza's empty cabin.

Suddenly behind them, a twig snapped. A high-pitched howl cut through the quiet air. Mateo's heart thundered in his chest. He turned towards the forest, just in time to see a shape racing towards him.

The shape rammed into Mateo, knocking him to the ground!

Chapter Eight

A CLOSER LOOK

Mateo landed hard in the dirt. The shape fell beside him, their legs tangling.

"Ahh!" the shadowy figure shouted. "It's the were-squatch! It's got me!"

Lola shined her torch at the shape. "Conner?" she said. Lying on the ground beside Mateo was the Australian boy, who threw up an arm to shield his eyes from the glare of the torch.

"Sorry." Lola clicked off the light.

"Are you following us?" Mateo asked. He stood, brushing dirt from his jeans while Lola pulled Conner to his feet.

"Yes. I mean . . . no! I thought I heard the were-squatch," Conner said. "Then I saw it! In the woods. A big monster walking down the path."

"You're just trying to scare us," Lola said.

Conner made a cross with his finger over his heart. "No joke," he said. "You gotta get somewhere safe." Then he dashed off towards his and Mateo's cabin.

For a moment, Mateo and Lola stood in silence. Then Lola said, "You want to join him? Or do you still think it's a game?"

"Let's check out Reza's cabin," Mateo said. "But first, we have to make a pit-stop."

They quickly ran to the mess hall and

slipped inside the kitchen door. After finding the item Mateo needed, they headed to Reza's cabin.

Mateo first looked at the shrinking red footprints. The paint had dried, making the prints look cracked and faded. But there was still something off about them. "These prints," he said. "They look too perfect. If Reza was running from something, they'd be more splattered. These look like . . ."

". . . like they've been purposely painted?" Lola asked. She shined her torch at a small table, where a jam jar sat almost hidden. It was half-filled with pinkish water, and a paintbrush stuck out of it.

"Interesting," Mateo said. He walked to the window, reaching into his pocket for the item from the kitchen. It was a small zip-tight bag of flour. He opened the bag and carefully scooped some flour into his palm.

"I saw this on a detective show once," he said. Stepping up to the window, Mateo blew the flour from his hand across the window. Several smudges and fingerprints were revealed across the lower pane.

"What does that mean?" Lola asked.

"Someone messed with the window."

He pushed one finger against the glass; it wobbled unevenly. The line of putty along the inside edge was nearly gone. But the putty outside looked clumsy and thick.

Mateo closed his eyes to think. The clues were there, but they were scattered like the pieces of a puzzle.

How do they fit together? he wondered. He shuffled the clues in his head, trying to fit one into the next. And then he had it!

"I know what happened!" he exclaimed.

But before Mateo could say anything more, Lola let out a gasp.

"Mateo, look!" she hissed. She clicked off her torch and pointed to the cabin door.

Mateo followed her lead and clicked off his torch, too. In the darkness, a big shadow passed by the open door.

A deep, rumbling growl drifted in from outside. It made the hairs on Mateo's neck stand on end.

Mateo and Lola huddled together as the creature outside stalked back and forth.

"How is this part of the game?" he whispered to himself. "The were-squatch has to be real."

Mateo suddenly felt less confident about solving the mystery.

He could feel Lola shaking in fright. It seemed she finally believed the campfire tale.

The two friends huddled together in fear. But a minute later, the growling shape seemed to disappear. Mateo tiptoed to the door and peered out. The coast was clear.

"Let's go!" He and Lola made a mad dash from the cabin. As they did, a loud howl echoed through the woods.

"Where do we go?" Lola asked, panicked.

Mateo thought hard as another howl tore through the quiet night. He skidded to a stop.

"What?" Lola asked.

"Remember what Reza said before? Sometimes, a person runs *towards* what they're afraid of, not *away* from it," Mateo said. "He was giving us a clue. This way!"

Without thinking, Mateo clicked on his torch and ran straight into the woods. *Towards* the sound of the howls. He raced down the path, Lola at his heels. Ahead, the path split in two. Mateo cast the beam of his torch to the left – right at the hulking creature that stood directly in their path!

"It's the were-squatch!" Lola shrieked.

But Mateo ignored it and ran down the other path. Lola followed. The creature lumbered after them. Ahead, Mateo could see the narrow patch of ground leading to the shack on the lake. The two kids ran out onto the path, water on either side of them.

"I hope I'm right about this," Mateo whispered.

They reached the shack and turned around. The creature behind them blocked their way off the island.

They were trapped!

HAVE YOU SOLVED
THE MYSTERY?

What we know:

- Reza Amari mysteriously disappeared from a cabin that was locked from the inside.

- Weird shrinking footprints were found inside Reza's cabin. But Mateo and Lola discovered that someone had painted the prints on the floor.

- A remote speaker in the woods looks like a fallen tree.

- Lola recognized one of the police officers as an actor from a TV soap opera.

- In the supply shed, Mateo and Lola found a can of putty that had recently been used.

- The two friends also found several fingerprints on the window inside Reza's cabin.

Do you know how Reza disappeared from inside a locked cabin? Who painted the footprints on the cabin floor, and why? Who or what is the big beast that's chasing Mateo and Lola? Have you worked out the answers to this creepy mystery?

Chapter Nine

WHAT A TWIST!

"Run towards what you fear!" Mateo
suddenly shouted and charged at the creature.
It growled and raised its claws. Mateo bent
forward and slammed into the beast.

They both fell to the stony path. The
creature's head went sailing through the air,
bouncing on the ground and rolling away.

"Ooooooh," the creature said groggily.

"Mateo!" Lola cried out. She ran over to
help him to his feet and shone the torch on the

fallen were-squatch. But it wasn't a creature after all. It was a man in a costume. And not just any man.

"Mr Maxwell?" Lola blurted out.

"Ha!" Mateo pumped a fist. "I was right!"

"You know, you're quite strong for such a short boy," Mr Maxwell said.

"The were-squatch isn't a real creature at all," Mateo explained.

"You could have just said that instead of running me over," Mr Maxwell joked, getting to his feet. "Well, if you worked *me* out, then you must know that—"

"Reza's in the shack, isn't he?" Mateo asked.

Mr Maxwell smiled back. "Come on out, Reza!" he bellowed.

The shack door creaked open, and the missing boy emerged. He held a sandwich in one hand and a walkie-talkie in the other.

Behind him, Mateo could see inside the shack. There was a large-screen TV and a video game console attached to it.

Pretty nice set-up for someone who faked his disappearance, Mateo thought.

When Reza saw Mateo and Lola, he said, "I had a feeling you two would be the ones to find me! How'd you work it out?"

Mateo rattled off the list of clues he and Lola had discovered. "First, there were the fake police officers. They were actors, including a pretty famous one from *Where The Wind Blows*."

Mr Maxwell guffawed. "Never thought a kid would catch that," he said.

"The campfire story was obviously fake," Mateo continued. "The howls actually came from a speaker hidden in the forest. They were probably triggered by a remote control."

"I had one in my pocket the whole time," Mr Maxwell confirmed.

"The footprints were painted to look like they shrank to nothing. But you actually got out of the cabin through the window," Mateo said, turning to Reza. "You removed one of the window panes and stuck your arm through to lock the window. Then you replaced the glass with putty. Am I right?"

Reza smiled. "Now *that* was tricky to do. Especially after a storm!"

"Then after sneaking out the window, you hid here in the shack on the lake. Even though you claimed to be deathly afraid of water."

"You ran *towards* the thing you feared," Lola added.

"Bingo." Mateo puffed out his chest. "So how'd we do?"

"How'd you do?" Mr Maxwell used one

claw-like hand to wipe his forehead. "Why, you made renting this costume and sweating in it all night worth every penny!"

*   *   *

The following morning, after a peaceful night of sleep, Mr Maxwell gathered the kids together. They all gasped when Reza appeared beside him.

Mr Maxwell motioned for Mateo and Lola to join him. "Congratulations to Mateo Rivera and Lola Evans, the winners of this year's *TWIST!* puzzle competition!"

The crowd of kids broke out in applause. Mateo smiled and waved. He thought back to the moment he stepped off the coach at Camp Enigma and what Mr Maxwell told them when he first met the group.

The camp director *had* been right. It truly had been an unforgettable weekend!

GLOSSARY

accent tone or pattern of speaking used by people from a particular region

confident sure of oneself and one's abilities

inspection process of looking over or reviewing something

investigate gather facts and information to solve a mystery or answer a question

legend story passed down through the years that may not be completely true

ransack search a place thoroughly and forcefully

IT'S POSSIBLE

WHAT'S IN THE WOODS?

Scary stories are often told around campfires in the middle of a dark forest. But do unknown creatures really hide behind those trees? Is there evidence that woodland monsters actually exist?

In one case, pictures of a mysterious wolf-like beast were taken in the streets of Totoras, Argentina. Many people claimed it was an actual werewolf. But some thought it looked a lot like the creature from a popular film. Someone used computer software to place pictures of the beast from the film into street pictures of Totoras.

Chupacabra is Spanish for "goat sucker". Several people have reported seeing the hungry, red-eyed monster prowling the woods and small towns of Central America and Florida, USA. It supposedly leaves victims such as cows and dogs completely drained of blood. Madelyne Tolentino of Puerto Rico reported seeing the beast. She claimed it walked on two legs, had glowing eyes and had spines sticking out from its back. But this description matches the monster from the horror film *Species*. Ms Tolentino had seen the film, and her imagination did the rest.

Is there a lesson to be learned? Yes! Don't watch scary films before camping in the woods. Then you might not see scary creatures in the forest like the bloodthirsty were-squatch!

DISCUSS IT

1. Several times in this story characters said, "Run *towards* what you fear." What do you think this means? Would you run towards something that scares you? Explain your answer.

2. Have you ever gone camping in the woods and heard strange sounds at night? Was it a wild animal? Or was it just your imagination playing tricks on you?

3. Imagine you are one of the contestants at the International *TWIST!* Competition. What type of mental challenge would you be best at? Describe the kinds of puzzles or problems you think you could solve easily.

WRITE IT

1. The were-squatch could supposedly shrink its victims until they disappeared. Try creating your own scary monster that lives in the woods. Does it have similar magical abilities? Write down a description of it to share with your friends.

2. Try holding your own mental challenge competition. Ask some friends to write down their favourite riddles, puzzles and brain teasers. Then take turns trying to solve each other's challenges. The person who solves the most wins!

ABOUT THE AUTHOR

Brandon Terrell is the author of numerous children's books. He has written several titles in the Michael Dahl Presents, Jake Maddox Graphic Novels and Snoops, Inc. series. When not hunched over his laptop, Brandon enjoys watching films and TV, reading, watching and playing baseball, and spending time with his wife and two children at his home in Minnesota, USA.

ABOUT THE ILLUSTRATOR

Eugenia Nobati was born in 1968 in Buenos Aires, Argentina, where she still lives with her family, two cats and a dog. Eugenia started as a graphic designer in 1990, but in 1997 she decided to dedicate her time exclusively to illustration, mostly for children's books. Eugenia has illustrated everything from postage stamps to packaging to character designs for animation. Over the years, her work has been published in nine countries and more than 40 books.

The Lost Lenore

The Gulliver Giant

The Minotaur Maze

The Final Frankenstein

only from Raintree